HARPER
An Imprint of HarperCollinsPublishers

Zoomer's

Summer Snowstorm

Zoomer's Summer Snowstorm

NED YOUNG

Zoomer's Summer Snowstorm
Copyright © 2011 by Ned Young

Library of Congress Cataloging-in-Publication Data

Young, Ned.
  Zoomer's summer snowstorm / written & illustrated by Ned Young. — 1st ed.
     p. cm.
  Summary: When a young dog's snow-cone machine fills the backyard with snow, his imagination runs wild and turns a hot summer day into a cold winter day.
  ISBN 978-0-06-170092-7 (trade bdg.) — ISBN 978-0-06-170093-4 (lib. bdg.)
  [1. Snow—Fiction. 2. Imagination—Fiction. 3. Dogs—Fiction.] I. Title.
PZ7.Y8753Zr 2011   2009049484
[E]—dc22   CIP
                                                                                      AC

Typography by Dana Fritts
11 12 13 14 15   SCP   10 9 8 7 6 5 4 3 2 1   ❖   First Edition

For Tod, an amazing friend who
also happens to be my brother

A gigantic thanks to
Maria Modugno for giving
my imagination a very long leash

"Hey, Mom!" yelled Zoomer. "It's really, really hot outside . . . can I have a snow cone?"

"On one condition," said Mom.

"I know," said Zoomer, "that I clean up the kitchen when I'm done."

Zoomer switched on the snow-cone machine and looked through the cupboards. *Hmmm, let's see*, he thought, *what flavor do I want?* After making his choice, he turned around and saw . . .

. . . his snow cone was now about three feet deep. *Uh-oh*, thought Zoomer. *I'd better get the mop!*

But after thinking about it, Zoomer decided to put on his hat and mittens and open the kitchen window instead.

As usual, the twins had something to say to their little brother.
"Hey, what's with the hat and mittens?" asked Hooper.
"Yeah," said Cooper, "it's like one hundred degrees out here."
"Not for long," replied Zoomer.

The hot summer weather suddenly turned icy cold as winter came pouring into the backyard.

"I'm t-t-t-telling," said Hooper, shivering.

"Why?" said Zoomer. "I already asked Mom for permission."

"To turn s-s-s-summer into w-w-w-winter?" Cooper said, his teeth chattering.

"How are we supposed to practice for our baseball game with this in the way?" complained Hooper.

"I guess we'll just have to play around it," Cooper said with a huff.

While Hooper and Cooper griped about the freezing weather, Zoomer got right to work taking advantage of the first snowstorm of the season.

After Zoomer had finished his snow sculpture,
he decided it needed some company . . .

. . . so he built his very own wildlife sanctuary filled with animals and creatures from near, far, yesterday, and beyond.

Later, Zoomer took a hot chocolate break in the polar empire of Zoomarctica and gave his brothers a friendly little wave.

"Don't look," whispered Hooper. "You'll only encourage him."

"You have to admit, though," whispered Cooper, "that is pretty cool."

"Toot! Toot!" shouted Zoomer.
"Hey!" said Hooper. "Can't you see
we're trying to practice here?"
But when Zoomer began building . . .

. . . an amusement park, their mittens went on faster than a happy puppy's wagging tail.

When Zoomer's tummy grumbled that it was close to dinnertime,
he scampered to the kitchen and cleaned up all the snow.

As Zoomer finished, Mom and Dad came in. "Zoomie," said Mom, "you look hungry. What would you like for dinner?"

"Chili!" yipped Zoomer.

"*Chili?!*" exclaimed Mom.

"Yeah!" said Zoomer. "On a really, really cold day like today, a big, hot, steaming bowl of chili would hit the spot."

"Well—okay then," said Mom, "chili it is."